Water-wise

Heather Hammonds

Contents

Water — A Natural Wonder   2

Earth's Water Cycle   4

When Rivers Flow   6
Case Study: The Nile River

Freshwater Lakes   10
Case Study: The Great Lakes of
North America

Dams   14
Case Study: The Snowy Mountains
Hydro-electric Scheme

Groundwater   18

Making Fresh Water   20

Conserving Water   22

Glossary and Index   24

NELSON
CENGAGE Learning

Australia • Brazil • Japan • Korea • Mexico • Singapore • Spain • United Kingdom • United States

Water — A Natural Wonder

Earth looks blue when viewed from space. This is because almost three quarters of our planet is covered with water.

Most of this water is salty sea water. Only a small amount of water on Earth is fresh water.

97% of Earth is covered in sea water. 3% of Earth is covered in fresh water.

fresh water

sea water

Water-wise!

Most of Earth's fresh water is ice. It is frozen in icecaps at the North and South poles.

All living things need water to survive. Some plants and animals can live in salt water, but many cannot survive without fresh water.

People need fresh water to survive, too. We can live without food for weeks, but we can only live without water for a few days.

Earth's Water Cycle

5 The water vapour meets cooler air. It condenses into tiny droplets and forms clouds.

1 Rain falls to Earth.

4 Warm winds carry the water vapour higher.

3 Water vapour rises.

2 Water evaporates and becomes water vapour.

When the Sun shines on Earth, it warms the seas, lakes, rivers and lands. Water **evaporates** and forms clouds. Rain then falls from the clouds and returns the water to Earth. This is called Earth's water cycle.

When rain falls, it flows back into the seas, lakes, rivers and lands. Then the water cycle begins again.

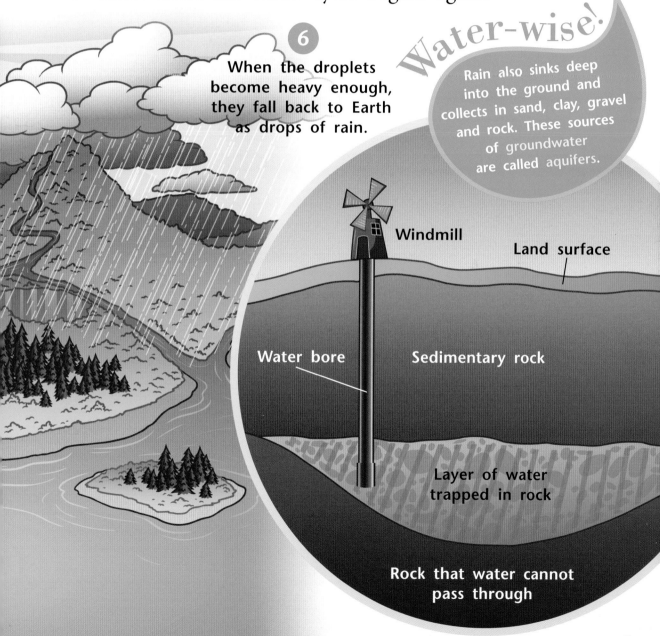

6 When the droplets become heavy enough, they fall back to Earth as drops of rain.

Water-wise!

Rain also sinks deep into the ground and collects in sand, clay, gravel and rock. These sources of groundwater are called aquifers.

Windmill

Land surface

Water bore

Sedimentary rock

Layer of water trapped in rock

Rock that water cannot pass through

When Rivers Flow

Rivers are an important source of water for people, animals and plants around the world.

Most rivers begin as tiny streams, high in mountains. As they travel towards the sea, other streams called **tributaries** join them.

After many kilometres, the rivers become much larger. As they near the sea, they often spread out and form a wide **delta** or **estuary**.

Water-wise!

Sometimes, after heavy rainfall, rivers flood. Floods spread silt from the river over the land. The silt helps plants to grow.

People around the world depend on rivers for:

- drinking water, for themselves and their animals
- growing **crops**
- transport
- trading goods
- fishing
- **hydro-electricity**

The Nile River

Nile River

Africa

The Nile is the longest river on Earth. The Nile and its tributaries flow through nine countries.

People have depended on the Nile River for thousands of years. More than 3000 years ago, ancient Egyptian farmers used its water to grow their crops. The Nile was also an important source of transport.

The Nile is also an important tourist attraction. Thousands of tourists visit it each year.

Today, countries along the Nile still depend on it as a source of water and transport. Dams have been built along the river. Many water craft travel along it each day.

Water-wise!

The Nile River has two main tributaries —the White Nile and the Blue Nile. Silt gives water in the White Nile a milky colour. Water in the Blue Nile is clearer.

The White Nile.

The Blue Nile.

Freshwater Lakes

Freshwater lakes are an important source of water for people, animals and plants around the world.

Lakes are large areas of water surrounded by land. They form between mountains, in **craters** and in places where there are low areas of land. Water enters and exits lakes by rivers and streams.

People depend on freshwater lakes for:

- drinking water, for themselves and their animals
- growing crops
- fishing
- transport
- trading goods
- hydro-electricity

Water-wise!

Lake Baikal in Russia is the world's deepest lake. Parts of the lake are more than 1.6 kilometres deep.

11

The Great Lakes of North America

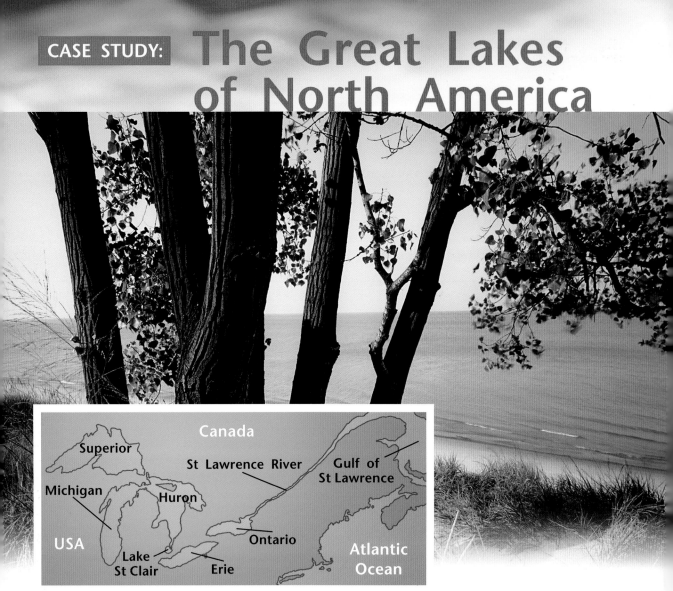

The Great Lakes system of North America is the largest group of freshwater lakes on Earth. Five lakes make up the Great Lakes system: Lake Superior, Lake Huron, Lake Michigan, Lake Erie and Lake Ontario.

The lakes are home to fish, birds and other animals. Millions of people live close to the shores of the Great Lakes.

Water-wise!

The Great Lakes system is so large that it spreads across parts of two countries — Canada and the United States of America.

Large forests grow at the edges of the cold northern parts of the Great Lakes system. In the warm southern parts of the Great Lakes system, the land around the lakes is farmed. Cities and towns have been built near the lakes. There are many factories in the cities and towns.

The Great Lakes are joined to each other and to the ocean by rivers and canals. Ships carry goods and people through these important **shipping lanes**.

Dams

Many people do not live near rivers or lakes. Dams are an important source of water for them.

Dams store water that comes from rivers and streams. A dam wall blocks the river or stream. Water builds up behind the wall and forms a **reservoir**.

When water is needed, it is released from the dam. The water runs through pipes, or into rivers and streams below the dam.

People depend on dams for:

- drinking water, for themselves and their animals
- growing crops
- hydro-electricity

Water-wise!

When a dam is full, water can be released through a spillway.

The Snowy Mountains Hydro-electric Scheme

The Snowy Mountains Hydro-electric Scheme in Australia is one of the largest groups of dams in the world. It is made up of sixteen large dams and seven power stations. The dams were built to provide water and electricity for millions of people.

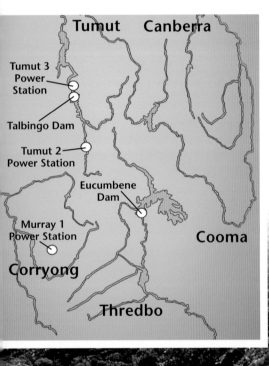

Water and snow from the mountains fill the dams. The water then travels through tunnels and pipes. It passes through the power stations, turning large turbines. The turbines drive generators, which make electricity.

After the water has been used to make electricity, it is released into two large rivers. Farmers use the water from the rivers to grow their crops. The rivers also provide drinking water for farm animals.

Groundwater

Groundwater is an important source of water for people, animals and plants in some parts of the world.

Groundwater collects beneath the Earth's surface in sand, clay, gravel and rock. When rain falls, it soaks into the ground, travelling down until it meets harder rocks that it cannot pass through.

Sometimes groundwater collects beneath the Earth's surface in large amounts. These reservoirs of groundwater are called aquifers.

Wells and **bores** are dug to reach groundwater. Then the water is pumped to the Earth's surface.

Farmers in many countries use large amounts of groundwater to grow their crops. In some very dry places, groundwater is the only source of water.

Many farms and towns in outback Australia pump groundwater from bores.

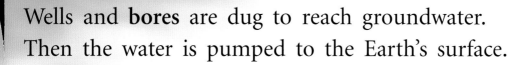

Water-wise!

The Great Artesian Basin is Australia's largest reservoir of groundwater. Some very dry areas of Australia depend on water from the Great Artesian Basin.

Australia

The Great Artesian Basin.

Making Fresh Water

Some parts of the world are very dry. They have very little fresh water. People must **conserve** their water supply. They must find ways of making fresh water.

People cannot drink salty sea water. But salt can be removed from sea water to make fresh water. This is called **desalination**. Salt water is specially treated at a desalination plant to make fresh water.

Water can also be recycled. Used water from sewage and drains is specially treated at recycling plants. Recycled water is used to water parks and gardens, to create wetlands, and grow crops.

Conserving Water

Clean, fresh water is the world's most precious resource. We cannot survive without it. It is very important that everyone tries to conserve water. Water can be conserved in many ways.

Conserve water in the house by:

- turning off the bathroom tap while you brush your teeth
- using a special water-saving shower head in the shower
- fixing leaky taps quickly — dripping taps waste a lot of water

Water-wise!

In some countries, there is not enough clean water. Governments and aid agencies work hard to provide everyone in these countries with clean water.

Conserve water in the garden by:

- using buckets of water to wash the car — never leave a hose running while you wash the car
- sweeping, not hosing, footpaths clean
- using **mulch** around plants to keep their roots damp, so they don't need watering as often
- watering plants at cooler times of the day in summer. The water will soak into the ground, rather than be evaporated by the sun.

Glossary

aid agencies organised groups of people who help others

aquifers large areas of underground water

bores holes dug or drilled into the ground to collect groundwater

conserve to save or preserve

craters hollows or holes in Earth's surface that sometimes fill with water

crops plants, such as grains or fruits, that are grown by farmers for food

delta the wide flat area of land and water at the end of a river, just before it meets the sea

desalination removing salt from water

estuary the end of a river where it meets the sea

evaporates changing from a liquid into a vapour. Water evaporates when it is heated, becoming mist, clouds and steam.

groundwater water beneath the Earth's surface

hydro-electricity electricity produced using the power of water to turn turbines, which drive generators that make electricity

icecaps large areas of ice that cover the North and South poles

mulch materials such as straw, which are spread around the base of a plant to help protect them and keep their roots moist

reservoir an area where water is collected. Reservoirs can be made by nature or by people.

shipping lanes areas of water where ships travel

silt sand, mud and earth carried along in water. Silt is often washed up on land at the edges of rivers.

spillway the part of a dam wall where water can spill out when the dam is full

tributaries streams and rivers that add water to a larger river, lake or dam

Index

aquifers 5, 18

conserving water 20, 22–23

crops 7, 8, 11, 15, 17, 19, 21

dams 9, 14–17

desalination 20

drinking water 7, 11, 15, 17

fishing 7, 11

floods 6

fresh water 2, 3, 10, 11, 12, 20

Great Lakes, The 12–13

groundwater 5, 18–19

hydro-electricity 7, 11, 15, 16–17

lakes 5, 10–13

Nile river 8–9

rain 4–5, 6

reservoirs 14, 18, 19

rivers 5, 6–10, 13, 14, 17

salt water 2, 3, 20

Snowy Mountains Hydro-electric Scheme 16–17

streams 6, 10, 14

trading goods 7, 11

travel 7, 11

water cycle 4–5